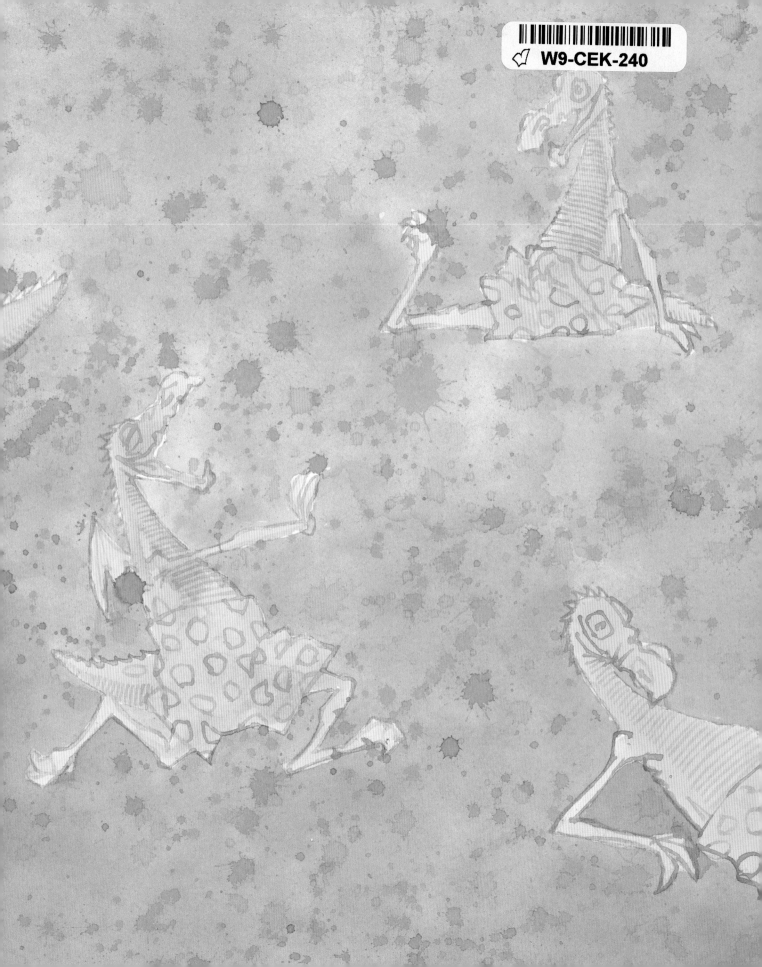

Morris

and the

Kingdom

of

Knoll

Story by T.L. Hill

Illustrations by Jeff Colson

The J. Paul Getty Museum *and* Children's Library Press

Morris was a dragon. A big, green, lumpy, bumpy, friendly dragon that lived in a big, dark, damp cave on top of a very high hill. Morris liked being a dragon and was quite content doing dragon things every day.

At the bottom of the very tall hill was the kingdom of Knoll, its king, many neat and tidy well-kept houses, and the hustling, bustling, happy people who lived there. Well, they were happy most of the time, but . . .

Every now and then Morris liked to charge down the hill,

KERTHUMP! KERTHUMP! KERTHUMP!

and

SPLASH

through the king's moat,

CRASH

through the surrounding kingdom walls,

SCARE

all the people and tear up the whole kingdom! It really was an awful mess.

(Because that's what dragons do.)

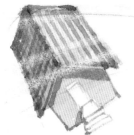

The people of Knoll were afraid of Morris. But, to be more exact, they were pretty tired and fed up with his dragon antics. Every time Morris would charge down the hill and crash through their kingdom, everything had to be fixed, rebuilt, and cleaned up.

The stone-layers would build new walls around the kingdom and lay new streets. The carpenters were busy night and day building new houses for all the people. And the sanitation department had to clean up the whole awful mess. The rest of the men and women worked in the gardens replanting their vegetable crops. The children had to carry tools to all the workers, take everyone food when they were hungry, and carry water to them when they were thirsty.

Then just when the people of Knoll had everything finished and their kingdom put nicely back together, Morris would charge back down the hill,

KERTHUMP! KERTHUMP! KERTHUMP!

and tear it up all over again!

(So, they complained . . .)

"We're tired of working day after day, week after week, month after month, and year after year, over and over again," they whined to their king. "You must do something!"

Indeed, something needed to be done. The king started immediately to think of a way to help the people of Knoll.

(Because the people of Knoll were good people.)

When evening came, the king chose a very brave person from among the people to climb the very high hill and quietly watch Morris.

"Hide yourself behind the rocks," the king instructed, "and let me know when Morris is in his cave and fast asleep."

The bravest person in Knoll did just that, and when news returned that Morris was sleeping soundly the king put his plan to work.

(He was a very wise king.)

The king chose the strongest people in his kingdom and sent them to the top of the very high hill with these directions,

"Roll the biggest boulder you can find in front of Morris's cave."

"That will keep Morris in his place," the king told the people. "That will keep Morris from charging down the hill and tearing up our kingdom."

(And it did.)

No more Morris. No more

KERTHUMP! KERTHUMP! KERTHUMP!

down the hill.

No more

SPLASHING

through the moat,

CRASHING

through the walls,

SCARING

all the people

and tearing up the whole kingdom.

The people of Knoll were pleased. They lived and worked in peace.

The stone-layers fixed all the walls and laid nice streets running through the kingdom. The carpenters built strong, pretty houses, and the sanitation department would clean the messes that they made. The men and women worked leisurely in the gardens while the children laughed and played. And everyone seemed quite happy. Well, for a while anyway . . .

Soon there were no more walls to be fixed. So the stone-layers began building new walls weaving them in and out through the kingdom,

round and round,

up and down,

silly, crazy walls

until they could build no more! The carpenters built so many houses there was not possibly room for another and there were no more messes for the sanitation department to clean. When everyone went to work in the gardens they were finished by noon!

The children complained, "We don't have anything to do."

(And everyone else joined in.)

Having no more Morris meant having no more work for the people of Knoll. They began to sit around idly. They became cranky. They became bored. And the happy people of Knoll weren't quite so happy anymore.

(So . . . they complained.)

"We've nothing to do!" they told their king. "No walls to fix, no houses to build, no messes to clean. And if we all go to the gardens to work, we're finished before noon."

The king, being wise
(as I told you he was),
knew exactly what needed to be done.

Again he sent for the strongest and sent them up the very high hill. They rolled away the big boulder that blocked the entrance to Morris's cave. As soon as they did, here came Morris charging down the hill and chasing them all the way.

KERTHUMP! KERTHUMP! KERTHUMP!
DOWN, DOWN THE HILL!
SPLASH THROUGH THE KING'S MOAT,
CRASH THROUGH
THE SURROUNDING WALLS,
SCARING ALL THE PEOPLE
AND TEARING UP
THE WHOLE KINGDOM!

The stone-layers had to fix the walls and lay new streets. The carpenters had to build new houses for all the people, and the sanitation department cleaned up the whole awful mess. The rest of the men and women worked in the gardens replanting their vegetable crops. The children carried tools to everyone who worked, carried food to them when they were hungry, and water to them when they were thirsty.

Soon the kingdom was put nicely back together and just when it was . . .

Here came Morris charging down the hill,

KERTHUMP! KERTHUMP! KERTHUMP!

and tore it up all over again!

But . . .

the people of Knoll were really quite happy.

(Because people are funny like that.)

For my Father, thank you.
T. L. H.

Text © 1996 T. L. Hill
Illustrations © 1996 Jeff Colson

The J. Paul Getty Museum
17985 Pacific Coast Highway
Malibu, California 90265-5799

Children's Library Press
P.O. Box 2609
Venice, California 90294

At the J. Paul Getty Museum:
Christopher Hudson, Publisher
Mark Greenberg, Managing Editor

At Children's Library Press:
Jerry Sohn, Publisher
Teresa Bjornson, Editor in Chief

Project Staff:
Kurt Hauser, Designer
Jack Ross, Photographer

Library of Congress Cataloging-in-Publication Data

Hill, T. L.
    Morris and the kingdom of Knoll / written by T.L. Hill; drawings
  by Jeff Colson.
        p.   cm.
    Summary: When Morris the dragon keeps crashing through the kingdom
  of Knoll tearing things up, the villagers go to the king for a
  solution.
    ISBN 0-89236-341-X
    [1. Dragons—Fiction. 2. Work—Fiction.]   I. Colson, Jeff, ill.
  II. Title.
  PZ7.H55744Mo   1996
  [E]—dc20   95-39556
                                                 CIP
                                                 AC